Fight in the Fields

Cesar Chavez

by Margo Sorenson

Cover Photo: Bettmann
Inside Illustration: Sue Bjork

Dedication

For Jim, Jane, and Jill, without whose unflagging support this book could not have happened.

For Carla, ever the encourager, including Rosalinda and her *churros*.

About the Author

Margo Sorenson was born in Washington, D.C. She spent the first seven years of her life in Europe, living where there were few children her age. She found books to be her best friends and read constantly. Ms. Sorenson wrote her own stories too. Her first one was called "Leo and Bo-Peep," which still makes her laugh today.

Ms. Sorenson finished her school years in California, graduating from the University of California at Los Angeles. She taught high school and middle school and raised a family of two daughters. Ms. Sorenson is now a full-time writer, writing primarily for young people junior high age or older. Ms. Sorenson enjoys writing for these age groups since she believes they are ready for new ideas and experiences and they really enjoy "living" the lives of the characters in books.

After having lived in Hawaii and California, Ms. Sorenson now lives in Minnesota with her husband. She enjoys traveling to Europe and visiting places she might write about. When she isn't writing, she enjoys reading, sports, and traveling.

9 10 PP 08 07 06

Contents

1

Detention Disaster

"Take it!" Aleesa hissed. She tossed the note on Kenneth's desk. What was wrong with him? He thought he was too good to pass notes. Aleesa made a face.

Kenneth frowned. The note lay on his desk. *To Tyleene,* it said. Aleesa had drawn flowers and hearts on it—again. He leaned back in his chair. He tightened his mouth. All Aleesa did was mess around.

"Now class," Mrs. Carter was saying. She turned to the board. "The migrant worker problem was getting worse in the sixties." With a purple marker she wrote, *Public Law 414.*

Boring, Aleesa thought. She slid down in her desk and sighed. B-O-R-I-N-G. Who cared about migrant workers anyway? People who picked stuff in fields. So they had a hard life. So what? So did she.

Aleesa glanced over at Kenneth. He was staring at the words on the board.

Public Law what? Kenneth asked himself. Did Mrs. Carter really think they'd learn this junk? Did she think they even cared?

Sure, he had to get decent grades to stay eligible for football. But none of this had anything to do with his life. That was for sure. He frowned and looked down at Aleesa's note. He should throw it back at her.

Aleesa made a face. Yeah, her life was tough. Especially now. Grandma was really mad at her. Just because she came home late from the mall. Grandma would ground her until she was 35.

"Migrant workers lived in shacks," Mrs. Carter said. She punched the purple marker on the board. "They made a dollar a day. Sometimes they didn't get paid. The labor contractors cheated them. So did many of the growers who owned the fields."

So let them find another job, Kenneth thought. Who cared? He sighed and glanced at Aleesa. She was drumming her fingers on the desk. She glared at him.

"Pass it!" she hissed.

"Kenneth? Aleesa?" Mrs. Carter's steely voice ripped through the air. Kenneth froze. Too late. Here came Mrs.

Carter. She was staring at the note on his desk. Her hand was already reaching for it.

Aleesa sat still in shock. Her mouth dropped open.

Mrs. Carter stood next to Kenneth's desk. She picked up the note.

Aleesa's heart hammered under her shirt. Now she was toast. Wait until Grandma heard about this.

"Passing notes again, Kenneth and Aleesa?" Mrs. Carter's voice dripped icicles. Her eyes bore into Kenneth and Aleesa.

"Um, no, um—" Kenneth stammered. He felt his face get hot.

"This is your homework, then?" Mrs. Carter asked. She began to unfold the note.

"No, wait!" Aleesa blurted out. Carter *couldn't* read it aloud.

Kenneth sat up. Forget it. He wasn't going to pay for Aleesa's dumb moves again.

"Ah, Mrs. Carter. It's not my note," Kenneth said. From the corner of his eye, he saw Aleesa stick her tongue out at him.

"Those who write notes are guilty. Those who pass notes are guilty too," Mrs. Carter snapped.

Great. Just great. Kenneth pressed his mouth into a line.

"I don't know when you two are going to learn," Mrs. Carter sighed. She looked at both of them. "I'm going to assign you to Saturday detention. Grounds work."

What? No way! Aleesa slammed her fist down on her desk.

Mrs. Carter raised her eyebrows. She frowned.

Kenneth darted a glance at Aleesa. Knock it off, he told her silently. That's just gonna get us more trouble.

"Not weed-pulling, Mrs. Carter!" Aleesa argued. She planned to go to the mall with Tyleene. And what about her fingernails? She looked down at them. They were just beginning to grow back after basketball.

"Aw, come on, Mrs. Carter," Kenneth began. Saturday morning was his time at the gym. He had to stay in shape for spring football coming up next month. Pulling weeds wouldn't do that.

Darn that Aleesa and her stupid note, anyway. He turned and glared at her. Aleesa made another face at him.

"I'm sure Berkeley Middle School will look much better when you're done," Mrs. Carter said. "Now focus on what we're doing, please." Aleesa and Kenneth watched as Mrs. Carter took the folded note. Plop. She dropped it in the wastebasket.

Aleesa felt sweat bead on her forehead. Whew. At least Carter hadn't read the note. But Saturday detention—pulling weeds? A boring social studies class? Grounded? What else could go wrong with her life? She slumped down. She kicked her foot against the desk leg back and forth, back and forth.

Saturday morning, Kenneth walked slowly into the school office. That jerk Mr. Moody was leaning on the counter. He smiled a nasty smile at Kenneth.

"Too bad, Smith," Mr. Moody said. "But the weeds are waiting. Where's your friend?"

Kenneth dropped down into a chair. "She's not my friend," he muttered.

"So why'd you pass the note?" Mr. Moody asked. His smile stopped just below his eyes.

"I didn't pass it," Kenneth said. He tightened his mouth. He wasn't going to get mad. Let Aleesa be the one who got mad. She always did. All it did was get her in worse trouble.

"Ah, there you are, young lady," Mr. Moody said. He showed all his teeth in a false smile.

The door closed behind Aleesa. She stood, a hand on her hip. Great. Moody was supervising today. Why couldn't it have been someone else? He was such a jerk.

"Yeah," she said. "I'm here," she grumbled. "But I'd rather be anywhere else."

Kenneth glared at her. You're the reason we're *both* here, he wanted to snap at her.

"You've got two hours," Mr. Moody said, straightening up. "Let's go. No lollygagging around."

Lollygagging, Kenneth snorted to himself. Only an old guy like Moody would use a word like that. That was sixties' talk. He buttoned his jacket. Even March in Berkeley was cold.

Aleesa and Kenneth followed Mr. Moody outside. He carried a blue water jug. Aleesa dragged her feet. She kicked a little rock. Ping! It hit against a trash can. Mr. Moody looked back quickly. But Aleesa just stared at the ground.

Kenneth sighed. Aleesa was going to get them both in worse trouble. He could tell. Why couldn't she just handle it?

They reached the maintenance shed. Mr. Moody unlocked the padlock. Inside, he picked up two trowels and two weed diggers. He found two pairs of gloves. Aleesa and Kenneth took them.

Aleesa held her gloves by the fingers.

"Sick," she complained. "They're dirty."

"That's what you'll be in," Mr. Moody said. "Dirt. Get used to it. Next time don't pass notes." He frowned. "And watch your attitude, young lady. Or you'll be out here for another two hours. Both of you."

He turned to Kenneth. Aleesa stuck out her tongue at Mr. Moody's back.

Kenneth shook his head at Aleesa. He shoved his hands into the work gloves. He'd be lucky if they got out of this in two hours.

"I'll be around to check on you," Mr. Moody warned. He gestured to the flower beds. "Start here. I expect you to have all this done and more." He handed them the blue water jug he had been carrying. Letters on the side read

BMS—for Berkeley Middle School, Kenneth thought. "Here. In case you get thirsty," Mr. Moody added sarcastically.

"Thanks," Kenneth said. Mom always told him to be polite. He'd better at least try to fake being nice. Maybe that would make up for Aleesa and her in-your-face attitude.

Aleesa just snorted. Kenneth. He was always so cool. Or he thought he was, anyway.

"Well, let's get started," Kenneth said. He walked over to the flower bed. He knelt down and jabbed the weed digger into the dirt.

"It's hard," he said. "It hasn't rained enough."

"Great," Aleesa complained. "That's just what we need. Digging weeds out of hard ground. And for two lousy hours too."

After pulling some weeds, Aleesa looked up at Kenneth. "It's cold out, but I'm thirsty," she said. "Where's that water jug?"

"Here," Kenneth said. He reached for the jug. He handed it to her.

Aleesa tipped the jug up. She let a stream of water run into her mouth.

"I'll have some too," Kenneth said. Aleesa handed him the jug. He drank.

Aleesa shook her head. Something wasn't right. The water tasted kind of weird. She blinked. "Hey!" she said.

"Everything's getting blurry."

Kenneth rubbed his eyes. "I feel kinda funny too," he said. "What's wrong? Was there something in that water?" His heart began to pound. What was going on?

He shut his eyes for a moment. Then he opened them. In shock, he stared. Aleesa was right next to him, all right. But the buildings were gone. Berkeley Middle School was gone.

They were kneeling in a huge field. Rows of grapevines surrounded them. Dozens of workers were weeding between the vines. They wore old, baggy clothes and hats. They had bandannas on their foreheads.

Aleesa stared too. She grabbed for Kenneth's arm. "Where are we?" she croaked. "What has happened to us?"

Kenneth felt his forehead bead up in a cold sweat. "I don't know," he whispered. "Where *are* we?"

2
Trapped

Kenneth's head felt light. His heart pumped. His hands clenched the trowel tightly.

"Aleesa," he croaked. "What happened?"

Aleesa's eyes were wide with fear. "I don't know," she whispered. She looked around. She could hear voices. The workers talked to each other. But it was a different language. "What are they saying?" she asked.

"I don't know. But it sounds like Spanish," Kenneth whispered.

As far as he could see, workers bent over the vines. They were pulling weeds. Old men, young men. Old women, young women. Children too. Kids their age.

The next row over, a man stood up. He held his back. "Aaaah," he said loudly. He rubbed his back.

"Get back to work," a harsh voice barked.

Kenneth's muscles tightened. Who was that?

Aleesa whipped her head around. Behind them, a few rows away, was a dirt road. A pickup truck sat idling. There was printing on the door. *Barker Vineyards,* it read. A man with a red face leaned out the window.

"Get back to work, you lazy Chicano," the man snapped.

The worker bent back down. He began pulling weeds.

"Holy cow!" Kenneth said. He stared.

"I'd punch him," Aleesa said. She doubled up her fists.

"That's not the answer," Kenneth said. He shook his head.

"Yeah, you might be a big football player," Aleesa taunted. "But inside, you're just afraid." She hid her face behind her hands and laughed.

"I'm not afraid. I'm just not stupid," Kenneth said. He cracked his knuckles. Aleesa always jumped into stuff without thinking. That's why she got into so much trouble.

Aleesa snorted. "Yeah, right," she said.

Kenneth watched the truck drive away. Dust billowed up behind it. Barker Vineyards, Kenneth said to himself. That was it! No. It couldn't be. But it had to be. His stomach churned.

"Hey, Aleesa! You know where we are?" Kenneth asked slowly. He stood up. "I just figured it out."

"Duh. In a field," Aleesa said. She made a face. She brushed her knees off and stood up.

"*¡Hola!* Hey, you two new here?" a voice asked from behind them.

Kenneth and Aleesa stared at each other.

"Uh-oh," Aleesa whispered. "We're caught now!"

"Just be quiet," Kenneth hissed. Aleesa had better keep her smart mouth shut.

They turned around. A young man about 19 years old walked toward them. He had a bandanna around his forehead. He wore a hat. Patches covered the knees of his pants. Heavy work boots peeked out from under his ragged cuffs.

"I said, you two new?" he asked, smiling.

"Uh, uh, yeah," Kenneth stammered. That was safe, anyway. He looked over at Aleesa. She stood staring, her mouth open.

"Right?" Kenneth said to Aleesa. He jabbed her with an elbow.

Aleesa blinked. "Uh, right," she said slowly.

"Mr. Owens said he'd get some more workers," the young man said. "My name's Luis. Luis Lopez," he said.

"Owens?" Aleesa blurted out. "Who's Owens?"

Kenneth shut his eyes for a second. Aleesa and her big mouth. She was going to get them in trouble. As usual. They had to get out of here. They didn't need any more problems.

A frown creased Luis's forehead. "Owens. You know, the labor contractor? That jerk? He hires workers for Mr. Barker, the vineyard owner?" He looked at Kenneth and Aleesa carefully. "Isn't that how you got here?" He stared at their clothes. "You're not dressed right for working in the fields."

"Ah, mistake," Kenneth said. He grinned weakly. "We—ah—didn't know we were coming here today." Well, that was definitely the truth, anyway. Aleesa rolled her eyes at him.

"Ah, I'm Kenneth." He pointed to Aleesa. "And that's Aleesa."

"Huh," Luis grunted. He shook his head. "I hope that's the worst thing that happens to you today," he said. "Wearing the wrong clothes, I mean. But it won't be the worst. Not here."

"What are you saying?" Aleesa asked loudly. Kenneth jabbed her side. She frowned at him.

"You are really in for a bad time," Luis said. He kicked the ground with his dusty shoe. "This vineyard is Barker's. He's one of the unfair grape growers. Some of the growers are fair—not many, but a few. Not Barker, though. Picking for him is the worst. And Owens goes along with it. Of course."

"What do you mean, the worst?" Kenneth asked carefully. He and Aleesa looked at each other. This was sounding bad. Aleesa felt fear cut through her like a knife. This was sounding worse than being grounded by Grandma.

"He makes you pay for a drink of water. There are no toilets in the fields. He'll sell you a sandwich for lunch. Don't buy it. He says it's meat loaf. But it's canned dog food," Luis said. He spit on the ground.

"Sick!" Aleesa exclaimed. "That's really sick!" She swallowed hard. What was going on? Why weren't they back at Berkeley Middle School?

"He pays us pickers almost nothing too. Just like other growers," Luis said. He yanked the knot of his headband tighter.

"So, why don't you go somewhere else?" Aleesa asked. "Why don't you get another job?" Kenneth jabbed her again. She jumped and made a face at him.

"You *are* new," Luis said. He stared at her. "Don't you know *anything?*"

"I know a lot!" Aleesa said. She put her hands on her hips.

Shut *up!* Kenneth wanted to yell at her. But he bit back the words. Maybe he could still save the situation.

"You don't know much about working in the fields," Luis snorted. "We have a saying. *¡Sal si puedes!* Escape if you can! There's even a *barrio* called that. It's not like we can take a bus and get a job somewhere in a city. Picking and working in the fields is all we know," Luis said. He lifted his chin. "But my family is good at it. We work hard. We save our money. Someday," he said, looking straight at Aleesa, "we'll own our own house. Maybe," he said more softly. "Maybe—if Cesar Chavez can help us."

Cesar Chavez? Kenneth wondered. Who was that? Why did that name sound familiar?

This sounded crazy, Aleesa thought. "Well, I just don't know—" she began.

"What Aleesa means is we need you to show us what to do," Kenneth broke in. He glared at Aleesa.

"You *are* new." Luis shook his head. "Like this," Luis said. He bent down. Using a trowel, he spaded up the dirt. "Get the weeds out. When the dirt is loose, it's easier. We have to weed the vineyards in the winter," he explained. "The vines are resting. But the weeds take food from the

18

soil and away from the vines. So we pull the weeds."

Thwack! Thwack! Thwack! His trowel scraped in the dirt between the grapevines.

Aleesa and Kenneth looked at each other. They sighed. Then they kneeled down. Two trowels lay on the ground. They picked them up. They began turning over the soil. Luis walked down the row a little farther.

"I'm not gonna weed," Aleesa complained. "I want to get back home!" She stabbed the trowel into the dirt.

"No kidding. We're going to have to get out of here," Kenneth whispered. "We'll have to buy some time, though. We'll weed while we try to figure out a way to get home." He yanked out a weed and flipped it into a box. "At least we're in California still. Maybe we can hitch a ride back to Berkeley. It's probably only four or five hours away."

"No kidding," Aleesa said. "But how?" The trowel flipped some dirt into her face. "Rats!" she said angrily. She brushed her face with her hand. She looked around. "Doesn't look like anyone here would drive us home. They're all too busy. They probably don't even have cars either." She sighed.

"Wait," Kenneth said. He stuck the trowel into the ground. He looked around them quickly. Nothing was there except vines and weeds. "I know! The jug," Kenneth whispered. "We gotta find the blue water jug. We'll drink from it again. Maybe that'll get us back." He yanked hard on a green weed. "That's how we got here, anyway."

"Come on, come on. No social hour," a rude voice yelled from two rows away. From between the vines, Kenneth could see the same man who'd yelled at them before.

"That jerk," Luis muttered, turning back to them from his place up the row. "He'll be sorry."

Aleesa jabbed her trowel in the ground. "I don't see why you don't just quit this," she said loudly to Luis. "This stinks!"

"Shhhh," Kenneth whispered. "You're gonna get us in trouble. Again." He pressed his mouth into a thin line.

Luis's face grew dark with anger. "You'd better listen up," he said. Luis shook his trowel at them. He got up and walked back to Kenneth and Aleesa. "You make me pretty mad. It's a good thing you're new here. You sure don't know anything."

Aleesa and Kenneth looked at each other quickly. Uh-oh, Kenneth thought. He felt his muscles tense. Then he and Aleesa looked at Luis again.

"You have to remember. We migrant workers have no education," Luis said. "We don't know how to do any fancy city jobs. But what we do is important. Without us, there would be no fruit in grocery stores. No one would have vegetables to eat. The growers need us. They need us farmworkers. But we need our dignity. Our rights—

like other workers in factories. That's what Cesar Chavez is trying to change."

Chavez, Chavez, Kenneth repeated. He *knew* he'd heard that name before. But where?

"So you're important. Then why do they treat you like this?" Aleesa asked. She lifted her chin. This didn't make any sense. None at all.

Kenneth poked her arm. He pointed to himself and to her quickly. He jerked his head toward Luis. Aleesa had better start thinking.

"I mean treat *us,*" Aleesa added quickly.

Luis looked around him. Kenneth and Aleesa followed his gaze. As far as they could see, workers dotted the vineyard. The sounds of digging filled the air. Snatches of soft Spanish drifted past them every now and then.

"The growers and the labor contractors bring in other workers, *braceros,* from Mexico. They'll work for hardly any money at all. Even less than we do. So, the growers tell us, 'Tough. If you don't like what we pay, we'll bring in the *braceros.*'"

"That's really unfair," Kenneth said. He tossed a weed over his shoulder into a basket. Oh, yeah. Now he remembered some of this stuff from the boring textbook. Migrant worker problems. No kidding.

But wait. Something wasn't right. He frowned. This

farmworker stuff was a lot worse than he thought it was. All this migrant farmworker stuff was supposed to be over with, wasn't it? All that was way back in the sixties. And who was Cesar Chavez?

Luis bent his head closer to Kenneth and Aleesa. "Things are changing. Cesar Chavez started a union for farmworkers. The NFWA."

Kenneth's hand froze in the air. Cesar Chavez! *Now* he remembered! His head pounded. No way. This couldn't be! His jaw dropped. Stunned into silence, he stared at Luis.

"There's a strike on," Luis was saying. "Since September. The Filipino farmworkers started it. We joined them. We call it a *huelga*—a strike. Some workers are walking out of the fields. They're refusing to work. If the growers can't get workers, they might sign a union contract. Then we could get more money." His voice rose a little with excitement. His eyes brightened. "Other rights too. There are union picketers. And there's a grape boycott going on."

Kenneth looked around them again. But everyone between the rows of vines was busy. People were working here. He couldn't see any picketers. His heart still beat fast. No. Please, no. This couldn't be. Dread filled him. He felt the blood drain from his face.

"There's a boycott of the big grower, Schenley, too,"

Luis went on in a low voice. "Cesar Chavez is trying to change things for us farmworkers. We may see Chavez himself tomorrow. I heard the NFWA might be picketing in this vineyard next."

"Boycott? What's a boycott?" Aleesa broke in. This was crazy. Something was really weird here. Kenneth looked kind of sick. What did he know that she didn't? Fear began to creep into her.

But Kenneth jumped. "Cesar Chavez?" he blurted out. "Grape boycott? Schenley boycott?" This was crazy. That's what they were studying in social studies. But that was in the 1960s. Cesar Chavez was dead now. How could they see Cesar Chavez tomorrow?

He stared at Aleesa in shock. They must be back in the sixties!

They were trapped!

3

What Now?

A chill ran down Kenneth's back. They *were* stuck in the 1960s! he repeated to himself. Blood pumped into his forehead. Now what?

"Yeah," Luis went on. "As I said, Cesar Chavez started a union a few years ago—the NFWA. National Farmworkers Association. A union for farmworkers' rights."

Luis gestured to himself with his thumb.

"It's a union just for us," Luis said. "The NFWA is trying to get us money and respect for our hard work. The union wants to get rid of the labor contractors too." Luis's

24

eyes began to light up as he talked, Kenneth noticed.

"Chavez wants to get more pay for all the farmworkers," Luis said. "He wants things for us that will give us dignity." Luis put his shoulders back. He stood up straighter.

Kenneth knew he'd better say something. His tongue felt stuck to the roof of his mouth. They were definitely in the sixties!

Kenneth took a deep breath. "There's a strike on? So why are *you* still working?" he asked. Luis seemed like the kind of guy who would walk off the job too. "Why aren't you striking too? Aren't you in the union? You sure don't think some of the growers or the labor contractors are fair, do you?" he asked.

Luis's face darkened. "My father. He won't let us join the union. Not yet."

Luis spit into the dirt. Aleesa jumped. Luis sure had some strong feelings. This kind of sounded like that boring old stuff in social studies. But that was so many years ago. Hadn't things changed any?

"My father says farmworkers got killed years ago for trying to fight the growers. And he says we need the work." Luis shook his head. "He keeps saying we need the money. Growers and labor contractors won't hire union workers. So a lot of people are still scared to join the union." Luis's frown deepened. He looked around carefully.

Then he went on in a lower voice. Kenneth and

Aleesa had to lean closer to hear him.

"Growers have sprayed pesticide at strikers. They've tried to run them down with trucks. They've shot at them too." Luis's hands balled into fists.

Shot? Aleesa swallowed hard. This was worse than pulling weeds at Berkeley Middle School, for sure.

Shot? Kenneth repeated to himself. Great. This was worse than he thought.

Luis went on. "So, for now, we're not in the union. But I want to be. The union and Chavez are the only things that can begin to change things for us. That and the union strike. Maybe the boycott too." He whacked his trowel on a post. Dirt flew off the metal.

Kenneth gripped his trowel tightly. He studied Luis's face. Luis really sounded upset.

"But even so, I'm not sure I agree with everything Chavez does," Luis went on. "Yeah, the union is a good idea. But the strike, the *huelga*, and the boycott are crazy ideas. He's into all this nonviolence junk. He doesn't believe in fighting back." Luis's eyes narrowed. "But I do." He thumped his fist in his hand. "When I join the union, my friends and I are gonna take care of these labor contractors. The growers too. They're gonna be sorry. Real sorry." He folded his arms. "We've got plans. They hurt us, so we're gonna hurt them. That's the way to get things changed."

Kenneth and Aleesa stared at each other. Luis pulled

his sombrero down on his forehead.

"Well, we gotta get back to work," Luis said. "Sorry I talked so much." He grinned at Kenneth and Aleesa. Then he walked back to his place between the rows of vines.

"We gotta get outta here," Aleesa breathed. "We gotta get home. And fast. A strike? Farmworkers getting killed? People are gonna get hurt? This is pretty scary." She looked at Kenneth.

"No kidding," Kenneth agreed. "And there's going to be big trouble too. That Luis is planning something bad. You can tell. Besides," Kenneth added. He took a deep breath. How was Aleesa going to take this? "This is worse than you think. A lot worse."

"What do you mean?" Aleesa asked. Her heart skipped a beat. Kenneth looked weird, as if he'd seen a ghost.

Kenneth looked at Aleesa, hard. "We're not just in the vineyards in the Central Valley in California. We're—we're back in time too."

His heart thudded under his shirt. Aleesa's mouth opened.

"Didn't you listen to Luis?" Kenneth asked. "Cesar Chavez. *Cesar Chavez,* Aleesa! Remember reading about him? The famous farmworker guy? Social studies? Aleesa—we're back in the sixties!"

"What?" Aleesa squawked. Her eyes widened. "No! We gotta get outta here! Where's our water jug?" Aleesa asked. "That's how we can get back—maybe." She took a deep breath. She looked down the rows. "See that tree right over there? It looks just like the tree where we started working at—"

Aleesa stopped. Her eyes filled with tears. "—at Berkeley Middle School," she said. "I . . . I just want to go home," she wailed softly. "I don't want to be a farmworker. I don't want to eat dog food. I don't want to get run down with a truck. And I don't want to live in the sixties!"

"Okay, okay," Kenneth said quickly. "Just be quiet. Come on. Let's hurry."

They glanced around for the foreman in the truck. But he was nowhere in sight. They hurried toward the tree.

"It was here. The blue jug. It was right here," Aleesa was saying as they got to the tree.

Kenneth looked on the ground. There was a round, damp place in the dirt. It looked as if a jug had been there.

But there was no jug. Now what would they do?

"No!" Aleesa cried out. She sank to her knees in the dirt.

"Shhhh!" Kenneth warned. His heart beat quickly. Maybe the jug was around on the other side of the tree. He looked. But the ground was bare.

He leaned against the tree. He stared at Aleesa. His mind felt frozen.

Aleesa was pounding her fists into the dirt. "No! No! No! This isn't fair! I want to go home!" she said. "I hate this! I hate it!"

Kenneth pulled Aleesa up. "Shhhh!" he said again. "Look," he hissed. "We'll figure out a way. Tomorrow we can find the jug. Maybe someone else took it."

Right, he thought. He didn't really think so himself. But he had to get Aleesa under control. Or else they'd be dust.

"Come on," Kenneth said. He led Aleesa back to their row. She snuffled and wiped her nose on her sleeve. Luis looked up. He shrugged and went back to work.

Dig, pull, toss. Dig, pull, toss. The sun lowered in the sky. Kenneth leaned back on his heels.

"This seems like hours," he said to Aleesa. The sky was growing dark.

"Where are we going to sleep?" Aleesa whimpered. "If we can't get back home, what can we do?"

"You don't even have a place to sleep?" Luis asked. He had come up behind them. "You *are* pretty mixed up." He shook his head again. But he grinned. "I don't know why I like you two, but I do. You're kinda crazy. But you can stay with my family." He tossed a weed into the basket. "We have room. My older brother and sister are gone. You can use their beds."

Aleesa looked at Luis's mud-caked clothes. Ick. She shuddered. What would his house be like? It was probably a shack. Why couldn't she just go home? She wouldn't even care if Grandma was going to ground her.

"Thanks," Kenneth said quickly. It sure wouldn't be the Ritz Hotel. Not that he'd ever been there. But at least they'd have a safe place to stay. Luis had a temper, but he was kind. He could see that in his eyes.

Luis went back to work. When his back was turned, Kenneth leaned over to Aleesa.

"It'll be safe. Then tomorrow we can look for the jug and get back home," he promised.

BWAAAAAAAAAAP! BWAAAAAAAAAAP!

Aleesa jumped. So did Kenneth.

"What was that?" they asked at the same time.

"What planet are you two from?" Luis asked, standing up. He brushed off his knees and grinned.

What planet were they from? No, what *time* were they from! Kenneth and Aleesa flinched. Aleesa bit her lip. Kenneth swallowed hard. They couldn't give themselves away or they'd be sent to the nuthouse for sure. Who'd believe them?

"That's the quitting horn. It's time to quit for the day," Luis said. "Come on. I'll take you to meet my family. You'll ride home with us."

The sounds of Spanish filled the air. Dozens of workers jumped into the backs of trucks. Engines sputtered to life. Trucks began pulling out of the fields. Dust clouds billowed up.

Luis led Aleesa and Kenneth to an old, faded red Plymouth parked on the dusty road.

An older man in a worn blue shirt, jeans, and work boots leaned against the car. He smiled at them. He tipped his sombrero to Aleesa.

"*¡Hola!*" he said.

"*¡Hola!*" Luis answered. "These are my new friends, Papa," Luis said. "Kenneth and Aleesa. This is my father, Juan Lopez."

"Hello," Kenneth said. He shook Mr. Lopez's hand.

"Hi," Aleesa said.

A woman with sparkling brown eyes walked up. "And here's my mother, Rosa," Luis added. Rosa smiled at Kenneth and Aleesa. She took off her sun hat and ran her fingers through her hair.

"Mama, these two need a place to stay. Is it all right?" Luis asked.

Rosa looked at Kenneth and Aleesa. "*Si.* Of course," she said, smiling. "Friends of yours are always welcome."

Whew, Kenneth thought. At least they could sleep tonight. Tomorrow they'd figure out how to get back home to Berkeley in their own year.

"Miguel and Jorge, the twins," Luis went on, as two boys of about 16 jogged up and climbed into the car. They nodded at Kenneth and Aleesa.

Doors slammed. Kenneth and Aleesa sat in the back

31

seat, squished between Luis and Jorge. Juan started the old car.

CHUG-A-CHUG-A-CHUG-CHURRRRR. The car pulled out onto the dirt road. Clouds of dust trailed behind it.

"Well, at least the car started one more time," Juan said. "Good thing. We don't have money to fix her."

"Doesn't this thing have a seat belt?" Aleesa asked. She fumbled around her on the seat. "Ooof!" she exclaimed. Kenneth had just dug a sharp elbow into her side. Why couldn't he just leave her alone?

"No seat belts yet, ding-dong," Kenneth hissed. "Be quiet, will you?"

Aleesa slunk down in her seat. This was going to be unreal. She already knew it. Trapped in another place *and* another time! A knot tied itself in her stomach.

"We don't have any money to fix the car," Luis repeated. He leaned forward. "We'll never have any money." He pounded on the back of Juan's seat. "If you'd let us join the union, maybe it would help," he said.

"*Mi hijo,*" Rosa said. She turned to look at Luis from the front seat. "Hush. Your father knows what he's doing."

"We're starving. We never can save enough money. We work like slaves!" Luis exclaimed. His fist banged against the top of the seat back. "Union is the answer. *¡La Causa!* Our cause!"

Aleesa looked at Kenneth. Luis could get really mad, she thought.

Kenneth shook his head at her. Don't say anything now, stupid, he begged silently.

"Listen, Luis," Juan said. His shoulders straightened. "Cesar Chavez is a good man. I just don't know if the union—the NFWA—will help us or hurt us. Remember, we need the jobs and the money. If we join the union, growers or labor contractors won't hire us. They hate the union." Juan looked over at Rosa. She nodded her head in agreement. "And we have to eat. If we strike, we might starve. The union doesn't have a lot of money to feed everyone. And we could get hurt."

Luis slumped down in his seat. Kenneth watched him carefully. His face looked grim.

"And don't forget what happened in Pixley," Juan went on. "Those farmworkers were shot for complaining."

Aleesa's eyes widened. She and Kenneth stared at each other. Shot? she repeated to herself. Fear prickled her scalp. Shot? Kenneth's brain echoed. He felt a chill of fear.

"The union will help us," Jorge chimed in.

"I think we should join," Miguel added. "Everyone is starting to join."

Juan shook his head. "I don't know where the NFWA will take us. Even though Cesar Chavez seems to be a good leader."

Tick-tick-tick. The turn signal clicked on. Juan steered the car onto another dirt road.

"*Sí,* Chavez is a good man," Juan repeated. "The grape boycott seems like a good idea. And especially the Schenley boycott. But I don't think boycotts will work. I don't think the boycott will force the growers to sign a union contract. Maybe not enough people will stop buying Schenley products. Besides, the growers have lots of money. They are too powerful."

"Will someone tell me what the Schenley boycott is?" Aleesa blurted out. She looked at Luis. *Boy*cott? Did it have something to do with guys? That might be kind of okay, if guys were in it.

Next to her, Kenneth sighed. Could they get out of this without Aleesa blowing everything? It would be a miracle.

Juan looked back at Aleesa in the rearview mirror. Everyone turned to look at Aleesa.

"You don't know what the Schenley boycott is?" Juan asked, surprised.

Luis stared at Aleesa and Kenneth. "You sure don't know a lot of things," he said. "Where are you from?"

Aleesa's eyes widened. Now what? she thought.

Great. Just great, Kenneth thought. Aleesa was going to get them caught yet. And then what would happen?

4
Join Up!

"Um, I . . . I ah . . . ," Aleesa stammered. She looked at Kenneth. Help me! her face cried out silently.

"We're not from around here," Kenneth said quickly. That was true! "She means she wants to know how the boycott's going," he added. "We haven't heard anything for a while."

Kenneth saw everyone in the car smile. Miguel and Jorge looked out the window again.

"Oh," Juan said. Kenneth could see his grin in the rearview mirror. "That's better. *Es mejor.* I didn't think there was anyone in California these days who didn't know about the Schenley boycott."

"Yeah," Aleesa said. She tried out a weak laugh. "That would be pretty dumb, huh?"

Kenneth sighed. Aleesa was something else.

"Well, it's going good," Juan said. "Cesar Chavez and the union picked a good company to boycott. Schenley is one of the biggest growers."

"Yeah," Luis said. "And one of the worst." He folded his arms. He leaned back against the seat.

Juan went on. "And you know they make more than just wine from grapes. They make alcohol and other drinks. Since the boycott is on, no one will buy Schenley products. Not until Schenley signs a union contract."

Huh, Aleesa thought. No guys, after all. Boycott— that meant no one would buy the things in stores. So why didn't they call it a *BUY*cott?

Luis sat up straighter. "Schenley is being hurt by the boycott too," he said.

Now Kenneth was starting to remember this stuff from class. He'd been so tired while he was reading the chapter for social studies, though. Mrs. Carter made stuff so boring in class too. Her lectures just about put him to sleep.

Juan nodded his head. "All over the U.S., people know about the boycott. Even outside California. No one is buying Schenley products. Not until Schenley lets union workers work for them."

"If only it would work," Rosa added. She looked hopeful, Aleesa thought. Rosa must lead a hard life. Work in the fields and then cook and take care of the family. Aleesa sighed.

The car pulled up in front of a small house. It was neat, but it needed painting. Someone had put geraniums in pots in front of it. But the front porch sagged. It looked like the migrant worker shacks she saw in those social studies videos Mrs. Carter had shown them. Oh, my gosh! she realized. This was the real thing!

"I'll tell you what will work with the growers," Luis whispered to Kenneth. "Not something wimpy like a boycott either." He slammed the car door hard.

"What?" Kenneth asked in a low voice. He looked around at the Lopezes. They were busy getting things out of the trunk. Rosa Lopez walked inside the house.

Aleesa walked closer to the two boys. She wasn't going to be left out of anything. That was for sure.

"No sissy stuff like Chavez does. If my father lets us join the union, my friends and I are going to change things. We'll do things that will get Schenley's attention. We'll make the growers notice. They'll be sorry they don't like unions." Luis slammed his fist into his open hand. "Very sorry."

Kenneth and Aleesa stared at each other. Uh-oh, Aleesa thought. Great, Kenneth told himself. Luis was a real hothead. Now he'd have to watch both Aleesa *and* Luis. He and Aleesa followed Luis into the small house.

After a dinner of rice, beans, and tortillas and some more talk about the union, it was time for bed. Aleesa turned and tossed on a cot in the kitchen. Kenneth shared a small room with Miguel, Jorge, and Luis. He slept on the floor, wrapped in a thin blanket.

The sky was still black when Juan knocked on their doors.

"*¡Vámonos!*" he called. "Let's go!"

They scrambled to get ready. Aleesa stumbled into the car last. The engine was already running. She tried to squeeze between Kenneth and Miguel. She shoved Kenneth over.

"Move over," she said grumpily.

"Fine," Kenneth snapped. He sighed and leaned his head back. He closed his eyes.

"What time is it, anyway?" Aleesa asked. She rubbed sleep from her eyes.

"Four-thirty," Rosa answered. "We have to be at the vineyard by five o'clock."

"Four-thirty?" Aleesa squeaked. "That's so early!" This was much worse than being grounded by Grandma. This was horrible.

"What time did you have to be at your last picking job?" Luis asked. He looked curiously at Aleesa.

Kenneth jabbed her side. "Aaaee!" she yelped. She swallowed hard. "I can't remember. But it was early too," she added quickly. Then she glared at Kenneth. He always thought he was so right. What a jerk. And here she was, stuck in the sixties with *him!*

The car drove down dirt roads in the darkness. The headlights picked out acres and acres of grapevines. The twisted vines stood out against the black sky.

"We're almost there," Juan said. "There's the gate."

He drove more slowly. Then he stopped the car. "Oh, no," he said. He looked through the windshield.

"*¡Huelga! ¡Huelga! ¡Huelga!*" voices outside the car chanted.

"*¡La Causa! ¡La Causa!*" voices echoed.

Aleesa and Kenneth stared out the windows. What was going on?

A small group of men and women stood on the side of the road. They held signs.

"Who are they?" Aleesa asked. She looked at the signs.

"The strikers. The union picketers," Rosa said. She sighed. "They don't want us to work in the Barker Vineyard." She looked anxiously at Juan.

Trouble. This could be trouble. Kenneth clenched his hands into fists.

Juan's shoulders slumped. "I was afraid it would happen here. I was hoping we could avoid it. At least for a while longer. I knew the union would come and picket this vineyard. Sooner or later." He looked around at everyone in the car. "Well, come on."

"What are we going to do, Papa?" Luis asked urgently. He leaned forward.

"Well, we will listen to what they have to say," Juan began. "They are our *hermanos*. Our brothers and sisters. We may join the union. We need change, after all." He sighed heavily.

"Look! Chavez! It's Chavez!" Luis almost shouted. "I want to hear what he says." He flung open the car door. He jumped out.

Kenneth's heart beat faster. There he was—Cesar Chavez! The car's headlights picked him out of the crowd. He looked just like the pictures in the social studies book and the videos.

Oh, my gosh, Aleesa thought. Cesar Chavez! He was smaller than she thought he'd be. He looked just—well—like a nice, ordinary man. He was wearing a plaid long-sleeved shirt, a cap, and jeans. He sure didn't look like he could beat anyone in a fight.

The chanting outside the car got louder.

"*¡Huelga! ¡Huelga!*" the people chanted. They waved signs.

Aleesa saw a red sign with a white circle in the middle of it. In the middle of the white circle was a black eagle. Other signs read *¡Huelga!* and *¡Viva La Causa!* The people moved the signs up and down.

Kenneth, Aleesa, and the Lopez family got out of the car. They stood in an uncertain little group, watching the picketers.

Cesar Chavez walked at one end of the line. He carried a sign that said *¡NFWA Unidos!* He chanted too. "*¡Huelga! ¡Huelga!*"

"*¡No esquiroles! ¡Esquiroles afuera!*" the strikers said. They walked up and down in front of the gate to the vineyard.

"What does that mean?" Kenneth asked Luis. "*Esquiroles* something?"

Luis was frowning. "It means 'no scabs, scabs stand aside,' " he snorted. "They're calling us scabs because we're working instead of striking. But I'm not a scab," he said in a tight voice. "And I want to join the union. If my father would let us."

"What's a scab?" Aleesa asked Kenneth in a low voice. She stood close to him. These picketer people didn't look angry, but you never knew what would happen. Especially with Luis around.

"A scab is somebody who will work and not strike. That hurts the strike. Because then the grower can hire scabs to work. He can still get his vines taken care of." Kenneth kept his eyes on the picketers and Cesar Chavez as he talked. "He won't lose money. So he won't give in to the union."

FIGHT IN THE FIELDS: CESAR CHAVEZ

"Shhh!" Luis hissed. "It looks as if Cesar is going to talk!"

The shouts of "*¡Huelga! ¡Huelga!*" faded. The people turned to look at Cesar Chavez.

"*Mis amigos,*" Cesar began. He looked at the Lopez family and the other vineyard workers who had joined them.

A hush fell over the small crowd. The sun began to rise over the horizon. Rows and rows of vines seemed to stretch for miles.

Kenneth felt a chill spread through him. He was actually hearing Cesar Chavez speak—in person! This was better than any social studies video, for sure!

Aleesa's eyes widened. What was Chavez going to say? A twinge of excitement ran through her.

"We are *hermanos*—brothers and sisters—in this struggle. We need your help. We farmworkers need dignity. We need a decent wage from the growers, not $1.20 an hour—and less. We need to be able to have a union hall where growers can come to hire us. We must get rid of the labor contractors who cheat us. They don't pay us our money," Cesar Chavez looked earnestly at every face in the crowd. He cleared his throat. "The peaceful strike is the way! Join your brothers in the union. We'll beat the growers our way. Sacrifice for our brothers."

"*No!*" Luis said loudly. Aleesa jumped. Next to her,

Kenneth blinked in surprise. What was Luis going to do now?

"But we have to get *back* at the growers!" Luis shouted. "We have to show them our anger!"

Some of the workers muttered. They shifted uncomfortably.

"Luis!" Rosa whispered. "Hush!" She looked worried, Aleesa thought.

From the corner of his eye, Kenneth saw Juan frown at his son.

"No!" Cesar answered calmly. He looked at Luis evenly. Then he looked at everyone's faces. "That is not our way. Nonviolence is the only answer."

Chavez's eyes became intense, Kenneth thought. Kind of like how he felt just before the quarterback's snap in a football game.

"Any fool can throw a punch. Or use a club. No strike is worth the life of a worker, a grower, or a child," Chavez said sternly. "It takes brains to demonstrate without violence."

The crowd of people began to murmur agreement.

"*¡Sí!*"

Kenneth watched Luis's face darken.

VROOOOOM! VROOOOOM!

Suddenly, a pickup truck roared up, spraying gravel and dirt on the picketers. *Barker Vineyards,* read the sign on the side.

"The grower!" Juan said loudly. "Mr. Barker! And Mr. Owens, the contractor!"

VROOOOM! VROOOOM!

The truck ran forward a few feet. The driver slammed on its brakes. Then the truck went backwards, then forward again. It stopped, its brakes squealing. More dirt and rocks were flung into the air and on the picketers.

Two men in boots jumped out. They carried rifles.

Aleesa's stomach tied in knots. She grabbed Kenneth's arm.

"Kenneth! Guns!" she said. Her mouth felt dry.

"Like I don't see them?" he answered back. His heart thudded.

"All right," barked one of the men. He held the rifle up. The crowd backed away.

Aleesa's grip tightened on Kenneth's arm.

Click! The man flicked off the safety catch.

No! Kenneth thought.

5

Trouble with Luis

"Now, look here," the man yelled. He looked at the picketers and Cesar Chavez. "You lousy union slobs, get outta here. I'll call the cops. You Chicanos," he said, looking at the group of workers, "you get to work. Sun's already coming up. You're losing money."

Kenneth kept his eyes glued to the rifle trigger. Thud! Thud! His heart beat. What if the man fired? The guy looked mad enough.

Could he push Aleesa out of the way in time? Could he dodge a bullet? Why was he unlucky enough to be standing here?

Aleesa kept a tight grip on Kenneth's arm. What should they do? Drop to the ground if the man fired? This was worse than a drive-by. Anger bubbled up inside her. This wasn't fair. Not at all. No wonder Luis was mad. No wonder he wanted to get back at the growers and the labor contractors. She felt like punching the guy herself.

Chavez just stood there calmly. He didn't move. He didn't chant. He didn't even wave his sign. Chavez and the other picketers just stood silently, watching the growers.

"Yeah, you think you can force me to hire union," the other man said. His face reddened with anger. "No union. Not here." He spat into the dirt. "Not at Barker Vineyards."

That must be Barker, Kenneth thought. He watched Mr. Barker walk around to the back of the pickup truck. Inside the truck bed, a huge dog barked. He strained at his leash. Mr. Barker untied the dog, still holding the leash. Howling, the dog jumped from the back of the truck. He almost yanked Barker off his feet.

GRRRRRRRR! GRRRRRRRR! The dog's teeth bared. Slobber dripped from his gums. He growled at the picketers. The leash tightened as he struggled to reach them. His paws scrabbled in the dirt.

This was just like that yucky movie about the monster dog, Aleesa thought. She backed away. Huge dogs were nasty.

"Get off my land," Mr. Barker ordered. Chavez and the picketers just stood there quietly.

Barker nodded at Owens. Owens raised the rifle.

Oh, no! Kenneth thought. He froze. Aleesa's hand was in a death grip on his arm. Was Chavez shot in the history book? Why couldn't he remember?

BLAM! BLAM! The rifle fired twice into the air. The dog yelped and snarled.

"Aiee!" Aleesa squealed. Kenneth clenched his fists. Next to him, Luis swore softly under his breath.

Cries of surprise and anger erupted from the crowd.

"All right, Mr. Barker," Cesar Chavez said. He stared at the grower. "But we'll see you again. You don't scare us."

Then he looked at the workers huddled by the gate. "Join your brothers," he said. "I urge you. Join *La Causa!* Come to the union office in Delano. We'll sign you up."

He motioned to the picketers to follow him. Together, they walked to two cars parked by the roadside. They got in. The engines started.

"Get to work, you lousy Chicanos," Owens snarled. He gestured with the rifle toward the vineyards. "You're not getting paid for standing around listening to slime like that." He pointed down the road in the direction Chavez and the picketers had gone.

Then he and Barker got into the pickup truck. They roared off. A huge cloud of dust filled the air.

It seemed strangely silent. A few birds chirped at the rising sun. Vapor rose in the air from the warming vines.

The little group of workers shuffled their feet in the dirt. They stared at each other. Some shrugged. Kenneth and Aleesa just watched everyone.

"That's it," Juan said forcefully. He looked at his family. "It's the union for us. I don't care that we have to work hard in the fields. But no one is going to call me a lousy Chicano." He shook his fist at the pickup truck in the distance. "Chavez will give us dignity. We'll join *La Causa!*"

"Yes!" Luis exclaimed. "*¡Gracias, Papá!*" he said, grinning. He shook Juan's hand.

The union! They were going to join the union! Kenneth thought. Wouldn't that be dangerous? The rifle shot still echoed in his head.

"How will we live?" Rosa asked softly. "We need to feed everyone. We need to pay rent for the house." She wrung her hands.

"The union has money. Not much. But Chavez always comes up with some," Juan said.

"The union is like family," Luis added. "Everyone helps everyone else. Many people all over the U.S. are sending money to the NFWA. Even churches." Luis smiled.

"Let's get in the car," Juan said. "I heard the union office is open 24 hours a day. It's time we joined."

The other workers watched the Lopez family walk back to their car. Kenneth and Aleesa followed.

"Now what?" Aleesa whispered. Her voice shook. "Do we join the union too? And how are we ever going to get back home?"

"We can't join the union. We're only kids," Kenneth snorted. "And I don't know how we'll get home. But right now, we really need to help the Lopezes. And all the farmworkers," Kenneth added.

"Those men were jerks!" Aleesa said louder. "No wonder Luis wants to get revenge on them."

"There are better ways to win," Kenneth said. "Weren't you even listening to Chavez?" He shook his head. Good thing Aleesa wasn't getting a grade for today.

Aleesa made a face at him. Kenneth always thought he was right. Always.

They got into the car and slammed the doors.

"To the union office," Juan said. He started the car with a jerk. "To join *La Causa!*"

He turned on the radio. A Spanish song played loudly. Trumpets and guitars blended in a melody.

"Yeah," Luis whispered to Kenneth and Aleesa. "Now to start some of *my* plans for the union. The growers will pay for what they do."

A frown creased Kenneth's forehead. "But Chavez himself said nonviolence is—" Kenneth began.

"Hah!" Luis snapped. "The Schenley boycott has

been on for three months. The strike has been on for six months. Have the growers given up? Has Schenley signed a union contract? Have we won yet?" Luis asked forcefully. "No. We have not. It's time for a change in the way the union does things," he said. He stopped and looked up. Kenneth followed his gaze. Rosa and Juan were talking in the front seat. They weren't listening.

Aleesa stared at Luis. He really knew what he was talking about, she thought. He was right. The strike had been on for a long time. And nothing had happened. That was wrong. She could still see the snarling dog and Owens holding the rifle. Her mouth tightened. Luis was right. The growers had to be taught a lesson. And she would help Luis and his friends do it.

Luis bent his head down again to talk to Kenneth and Aleesa. "My friends and I have plans," Luis went on. "We'll find others in the union who think like we do. We've got plans."

"But that's against Chavez and—" Kenneth started to say. Luis really had strong opinions.

"Chavez has done nothing. We will do something," Luis said. He set his jaw. He leaned back against the seat and stared out the window.

Kenneth shook his head. Luis was determined to do something. But what? It must be something violent though. Luis sure hated the growers.

Aleesa poked Kenneth in his side.

"Hey!" he said, turning to look at her.

"You should think about what Luis is saying," she whispered. "I think he's right."

"You're crazy," Kenneth answered. He frowned.

"Just wait," Aleesa whispered. "Just wait."

She watched Kenneth shake his head and stare out the window. Vineyards rolled by. The sky was getting lighter. They must be getting closer to Delano. Little stores stood by the side of the highway.

She was going to do something about the growers too. They shouldn't be able to get away with that junk. She would help Luis somehow. They'd get revenge on the growers. Forget Chavez and all the peace stuff he talked about.

And Kenneth couldn't find out.

6

Picket Poison

"*¡Bienvenidos!* Welcome!"

"More brothers and sisters to join us!"

The NFWA office echoed with the welcoming voices of a man and woman. They stood smiling behind a counter in the middle of the room. The Lopez family, Kenneth, and Aleesa walked through the union meeting hall toward them.

The counter divided the union hall in half. A steady stream of people came in and out of the union hall. Some read notices on the walls. Some talked to the people at the counter. Others stood in little groups and talked.

Kenneth and Aleesa hung back. They watched Luis, Juan, and Rosa fill out the papers.

"Look!" Aleesa whispered. She pointed to the walls. Kenneth looked. "Who are those guys in the pictures?" she asked.

Kenneth studied the posters on the walls. "I don't know. Let's look," he said. They walked closer.

"Pancho Villa, Zapata, Che Guevera," he read aloud. "They must be famous guys."

"They were all fighters for the common man," Luis's brother, Miguel, said behind them. "They all wanted freedom for their people." He began to read the notices on the wall.

Kenneth read some too. "Look, Aleesa," he said. "This notice says workers in factories get $3.50 to $5.50 an hour. But farmworkers struggle to get only $1.40 an hour."

"That's not fair," Aleesa said. She looked at another notice. "Listen to this. Anyone need help fixing your leaky roof? Call 455-3998. Ask for Carlos."

"There are a lot of notices like that up here," Kenneth said, reading on. "It sounds like everyone in the union wants to help each other."

"They have to," Miguel said. "They don't earn any money. They're striking. So they all have to help each other. And people all over the U.S. are sending money to the union. They send clothes and food to the strikers too."

Aleesa stared at Miguel. "You mean lots of people know about the strike? Besides in California?"

"*¡Sí!*" Luis's voice broke in. He had finished filling out his union papers. He stood behind Aleesa, Kenneth, and Miguel. "They all know. They know about the boycott too. But the growers still won't give in. And that's the problem."

"No kidding," Aleesa said.

"That's why I'm going to do something," Luis said in a low voice.

Kenneth frowned and folded his arms. Why didn't Luis just listen to Chavez?

"I don't blame you," Aleesa said. "And I—" She stopped, her mouth open.

Noise broke out at the front of the hall. Loud voices began talking. Kenneth, Aleesa, and Luis turned around. A group of workers clustered around the door of the union hall.

"Chavez!"

"It's Cesar!"

"*¡Hola, hermanos!*" the slightly built man said. He raised a hand in greeting.

Kenneth elbowed Aleesa. "There he is again," he whispered. He listened carefully to Chavez's words.

"We're going to picket another farm that grows grapes for Schenley Corporation. The Motinski farm. We heard they had workers there today. We need to go out there and picket. Now, everyone listen to the plan," Chavez said.

"Cesar Chavez is a real thinker," Juan said, coming up behind them. "We're going out to picket too. Right now," he added with a grin. "It's time we do something for *La Causa*—for our brothers and sisters in the fields."

"No joke," Luis grumbled. But he followed Rosa and Juan. The three Lopezes joined the group gathering at the end of the hall.

Kenneth and Aleesa tried to listen to what was going on. But Chavez spoke too softly. So they walked closer to hear.

"We'll go four or five to a car," Chavez was saying. "Follow my car. We'll caravan. Everyone carry one of the picket signs. We'll stand at the gate to the field. Then we'll ask the workers to leave the field."

"What if the grower comes? Or the labor contractor?" someone asked.

"Stand your ground. We'll be on public property," Chavez said.

"What if they have guns?" someone else asked.

The group fell silent. Kenneth felt goose bumps on his arms. Guns, again. These union farmworkers really faced danger. They were really up against it.

Chavez smiled gently. "Think for a moment. A man with a gun has a harder decision to make," he said. He paused. "You—the picketer—you're just standing there. You're just *there*. It's up to *him* to do something."

"Yeah," Luis whispered to Kenneth and Aleesa. "Right. It'll be up to *me* to do something. But not yet."

"But Cesar—" someone began. Kenneth looked over at him. The worker's face looked angry.

"There are no buts," Cesar said. "If we get violent, we lose. Remember, any fool can throw a punch. It takes brains to be nonviolent."

That made sense, Kenneth thought. Even in football, you had to think before you made a move on the field.

Another man shoved his way to the front of the small group. "Cesar, with guns—" he began.

"You must listen. If we fight back, every picket line would be a battle. And who would be stronger in the fight? Who would win? Who has all the money? The power?" Chavez asked. He folded his arms. "The growers. The big people. They would win. This is the only way *we* can win. No fighting back."

He looked at every face in the group. The man who had just spoken looked down at the ground. Next to him, Kenneth felt Luis cough angrily. Luis must not have liked what Chavez was saying.

Aleesa stood stock still. Maybe Chavez really had the right idea. People followed him. People liked him.

Maybe he was right about winning. Maybe he was right about how to win. It was kind of like her and Grandma, wasn't it? Grandma would always win. She had the power. And the few times Aleesa didn't fight back, things worked out. Aleesa frowned. Why hadn't she seen that before?

"Nonviolence is the only answer," Chavez went on. "We have time on our side. That's all we have. We must have patience. We must wait." He smiled the gentle smile again.

Kenneth stared at Chavez. He was really smart about people, Kenneth thought. Chavez made sense. Why couldn't Kenneth help too?

Impulsively, Kenneth tapped Juan's shoulder. "I . . . I want to picket too. Can I?" Kenneth asked.

Juan looked surprised. Then he smiled. "*¡Sí!*" he agreed. "I don't know why not. They have kids out on the picket lines too."

Aleesa's jaw dropped. "Hey!" she exclaimed. "If you're gonna picket, I am too!" She put her hands on her hips.

"Sure, sure," Juan said, smiling. "I know Chavez would be happy to have two more picketers." He looked up. Chavez was leaving the hall.

"*¡Vámonos!*" Chavez called. He strode out the door.

"Yes, let's go," Juan said. Kenneth, Aleesa, and everyone followed.

"I thought you were on Luis's side," Kenneth whispered to Aleesa as they got into the car. "I thought you wanted to fight back too."

"Not anymore," Aleesa said. "I really listened to Chavez this time. Just like you said."

"Huh," Kenneth grunted. He looked over his shoulder. "But I don't think Luis did," he added in a low voice. He shoved his hands in his pockets.

"I think you're right," Aleesa agreed. "We're gonna have to watch him. He might blow up."

Yeah, like someone else I know, Kenneth wanted to tease her. But he kept quiet and hid his grin.

Car doors slammed. Tired engines roared into life. Fifteen minutes later, they arrived at the Motinski farm.

His heart thumping, Kenneth grabbed a sign. *¡Huelga!* it read. Aleesa took one that had the NFWA logo on it, the black eagle. Here we go, she thought.

The others were already piling out of cars. Everyone had signs. They began to walk up and down next to the road.

Kenneth watched Luis. He walked with some young men to the end of the line. They walked slowly back and forth, holding signs. But they were talking together. Their heads were down. He saw Luis look around quickly.

"Hey, Aleesa," Kenneth said. Aleesa turned around. "Look at that," he said. He pointed to Luis and his friends.

"Uh-oh," she said. "Are you thinking what I'm thinking?"

"Yeah," Kenneth muttered. "I think we'd better try to find out what they're saying." He nodded his head to Aleesa and began walking toward Luis and his friends.

Aleesa hurried to catch up with Kenneth. "I hope they don't do something stupid. It'll wreck the good job the union's been doing," she whispered worriedly to him.

"I know," Kenneth agreed. "Chavez is so strong on not fighting back. He would be really upset. The growers would win for sure, just like he said."

"And all the sacrifices the strikers are making—" Aleesa began. She walked faster.

"Would be worth nothing," Kenneth finished, looking ahead at Luis and his friends.

"We'd better talk to him," Aleesa said angrily. "We gotta stop him." She held her sign up higher. "Let's get this over with. Now." She walked more quickly toward Luis.

Kenneth reached out a hand and grabbed Aleesa's arm. He sighed. Aleesa always jumped into things. "Look," he said. "We can't do it that way. He'll just get more angry. Then he'll really do something dumb. Let's find out what he's planning first. Then we can decide what to do."

Aleesa shook Kenneth's hand off her arm. "Okay," she said grudgingly. "I guess you're right."

Kenneth and Aleesa slowed their paces. They began walking back and forth in front of Luis and his group of friends. They tried to listen to the low voices in the group.

Suddenly, voices began to shout. An engine roared behind them.

"Hey! Look out!"

"It's Motinski!"

"Aiiieee! The spray!"

"*¡Peligro!*"

Aleesa whipped her head around. Kenneth stared. A big orange truck rumbled down the dirt road. A tank in the back of it was spraying something at the picketers. The picketers were scrambling, trying to get out of the way.

"What in the world is that?" Aleesa cried out. Her heart beat fast.

"A pesticide truck," Kenneth yelled. He pushed Aleesa out of the way. "I read about them. They're trying to spray us with pesticide—with poison!"

7

A New Idea?

"Poison?" Aleesa shrieked. She hid with Kenneth behind a shack. She dropped to the ground. The truck rumbled away. A man's snarling, red face looked back at them. All around them, picketers coughed and hacked. Some panicked and screamed. Some yelled. Some shook fists at the truck.

"I want to go home!" Aleesa wailed. "This is terrible!" She shook, huddled on the ground.

"Stop it!" Kenneth said angrily. He wanted to go home too. But whining about it wasn't going to get them anywhere. They had to think clearly. "We can't go home yet. We don't know where the water jug is. And don't you want to help the union and our friends?"

"See? See?" Luis's voice broke in. He and his friends had hidden behind the shack too. His voice shook with anger. "See what they do to us? This is why we have to do something." He stared at the retreating truck. He shook his fist at it. "Growers have shot at us! They've run us down with their trucks. Some *hermanos* have been hurt! We must show them we have pride!" he yelled. "Nothing will change until we do!"

"*¡Sí!*"

"*¡Es verdad!*"

"*¡No estamos locos!*"

Luis's friends' shouting filled the air. It was joined by the voices of the picketers. They were shouting angrily too.

"No, no!" a strong voice called out. Kenneth and Aleesa turned to look. Cesar Chavez stood in front of the picketers. He held his arms out at his sides, palms up.

"Don't you see?" he asked. "They're just trying to get you mad. They want you to fight back. Then people will be on *their* side." Chavez shook his head. "The growers are worried about their business. About making money. They can't get enough workers in the vineyards. Right now, no one is buying Schenley products either. They're losing money. They'll have to sign a union contract. They'll let union members work—if we are patient. If we wait. We can't fight back. People will think we're wrong. They'll side with the growers. We must wait."

Chavez looked at the faces in the group. He wiped his brow with his bandanna. Could Luis wait? Kenneth wondered. He looked at Aleesa. She raised her eyebrows. She jerked her head in Luis's direction. Kenneth looked over at Luis. Luis was scowling.

"Right now, the newspapers are on our side," Chavez went on. "They say we are peaceful. Even when the other side sprays us with poison, we are peaceful. Even when growers try to run us down with their trucks, we are peaceful. The public respects us. People think we are right. But if we get violent, no one will have sympathy for us. They will think the growers are right instead. Then we lose. The growers will never sign a contract. All our sacrifices will be for nothing," he finished.

The group shuffled their feet. Some people murmured. Others whispered.

"*Sí,*" one woman said. "You are right, Cesar," She tugged at the sleeve of the man standing next to her.

"Yes, Cesar," the man said. "We'll stay behind you."

Murmurs of agreement filled the air. The group looked at Chavez, waiting.

"We continue," Chavez went on. He picked up his picket sign. He began to walk up and down again. Slowly, the other picketers straggled into line. The picketers began walking.

Aleesa and Kenneth stood still. They tried not to look at Luis. He and his friends stood close together. Then they walked around the corner of the shack. Kenneth motioned to Aleesa to follow. They stepped quietly over to the shack.

"Listen!" Kenneth whispered to Aleesa. He tensed his muscles. They had to hear this. They could hear only snatches of words.

"—rocks!"

"—gunpowder!"

"—set fire to—"

Aleesa's eyes widened. She started to open her mouth. This sounded dangerous.

"Shhhh!" Kenneth whispered. Aleesa had better keep quiet. They had to hear Luis's plans.

"Hey!" Luis's voice in their ears made them both jump. Luis had walked around the other corner of the shack. He frowned at both of them. His friends joined him. They stared at Kenneth and Aleesa from under lowered brows.

"If you heard anything," Luis said, "you'd better shut up. If you say anything to anyone—" Then he stopped. He took his fist and ground it into his other palm. "You'll be sorry. You are my friends, true. But I must do what I have to do."

His friends muttered behind him. They looked scary, Kenneth thought. He looked over at Aleesa. She'd better not pick right now to tell Luis off about violence. Luis was okay—until he started talking about this union stuff.

Aleesa's eyes were huge. She just stared at Luis. Kenneth was right. It was too dangerous to say anything yet. They'd have to stop Luis somehow. But not now. Then she opened her mouth.

"Uh, no problem," Aleesa said quickly. "Let's get back and picket, Kenneth," she said. She grabbed Kenneth's arm. They walked to the picket line. The others marched back and forth.

"Here come the new workers," someone shouted.

A big, dusty bus drove up. Workers in shabby clothes began getting off. They saw the picketers lined up by the side of the road. Their eyes blinked in surprise. The picketers began to yell at them.

"*¡Huelga!*"

"Join your *hermanos!*"

"*¡Huelga! ¡Tenemos una huelga aquí!*"

Aleesa saw Chavez walk up to one of the workers. He was explaining something in Spanish. The worker's eyes grew large. Then he looked sad. The worker began to speak to the others in rapid Spanish. Everyone began to talk fast. Some shouted. Some waved their arms. They looked angry.

She saw Juan and Rosa nearby. They would know what Chavez was saying. "Let's ask Juan and Rosa what's going on," she said to Kenneth. Together, they walked up to Juan and Rosa.

"What did Mr. Chavez say to that man?" Aleesa asked. Juan held his picket sign still. Rosa stopped too.

"These are *braceros,*" Juan explained. "Workers from Mexico. The growers are using them to break the strike. They're brought up here from Mexico. Across the border. The growers say they need *braceros* to work the fields." Juan gestured to the fields around them.

Aleesa and Kenneth looked at the fields stretching away in the distance. A lot of workers were needed to work on the vines.

"The growers say they can't get anyone else to work. But that's a lie." Juan's face darkened. "We would work—if we were paid a decent wage. Chavez is telling the *braceros* that they're strikebreakers. They didn't know there was a strike, of course. So now they have to decide if they're going to stay and work. They have no money to get back home. Only if they work can they get a bus ride home."

"It's very sad," added Rosa. She looked up at Juan.

"That's really unfair," Kenneth blurted out. He stared at the workers milling around. They talked and gestured to each other worriedly.

"How can they do that?" Aleesa asked. This wasn't right.

"Now you know another reason why farmworkers need a union," Juan said. He began to walk up and down again. Rosa followed.

A lot of the *braceros* began to straggle into the fields. They hung their heads down. Aleesa noticed they wouldn't look at any of the picketers. They were probably embarrassed. But how else would they get home? How would she and Kenneth get home?

Kenneth saw three of the *braceros* talking to Chavez. Chavez was smiling. Then the three *braceros* got back on the bus.

"What are they going to do?" Kenneth asked Juan. Juan smiled too.

"It looks like they're not going to work," he said. "They'll ride back to the labor camp. Then they'll try to get home somehow. But they won't break a strike."

"It's not enough," Luis said in a low voice behind Kenneth. Kenneth turned around. Luis and his friends stood in a tight circle behind him. "Only three *braceros* refusing to work isn't going to make the growers sign a contract." Luis's friends nodded their heads in agreement. They folded their arms across their chests. "The boycott hasn't worked yet either. We need to get the growers' attention. And get it fast."

Kenneth and Aleesa looked at each other. Aleesa opened her mouth to say something. Kenneth frowned and shook his head. She shut her mouth and made a face at him.

"Okay, *hermanos!*" Chavez's voice rose above the crowd. "*¡Nosotros venceremos!* We will overcome! Let's go to the union hall. We have more work to do. We'll hand out leaflets about the Schenley boycott. We'll hand them out at supermarkets in Delano. There's something else too." He smiled broadly at everyone. "We have a new idea for the union. We think we have a way to get the growers to sign a contract. We think we can win."

Aleesa and Kenneth looked at each other.

"What do you think it is?" Aleesa asked. She began walking to the Lopez's car with Kenneth. "What could Chavez and the other union leaders be planning?"

"I don't know," Kenneth answered. He glanced over at Luis and his friends. "I just hope it will make Luis change his mind about what he's planning."

Everyone hurried to the caravan of cars. Picket signs were tossed into trunks. Engines started. One by one, the cars pulled out onto the dusty road.

Inside the Lopez's car, Luis stared ahead angrily.

"Handing out leaflets about the boycott won't make the growers sign. So Chavez has a new idea," he spat out. "We'll see. It had better be a good one. I'm tired of waiting," he said.

Kenneth shot a quick glance at Aleesa. Luis was right about that. Chavez's idea had better be good. Or there was going to be trouble. Luis would make sure of that.

What could Chavez's idea be?

8

Luis's Lie

"Handing out boycott leaflets all day wasn't easy," Kenneth whispered to Aleesa. It was later that night. They sat together in the union hall. The red NFWA flag with the black eagle hung on the front wall. The flag of Our Lady of Guadalupe stood at the side. The United States flag did too.

Dozens of people filled rows of folding chairs. Workers in faded jeans, work shirts, and sombreros packed the room. Many leaned against the walls. Some even sat on the floor. Everyone waited for Chavez to speak.

"No kidding," Aleesa said, making a face. "I'd almost rather be in Carter's boring social studies class. Did you hear what that lady said to me at Smith's Food King?"

"No. What?" Kenneth asked. He glanced around him. Everyone else was talking too.

"She said, 'If your family were growers, you'd know the strikers were wrong. Not all the growers are bad. You should stop this boycott. You should stop the strike. Or we'll *all* starve.'" Aleesa sighed. "Then she told me that Communists weren't welcome in Delano. She told me to get out of town!" Aleesa complained. "Why did she think I was a Communist, anyway?"

"I know," Kenneth said. "It was in our textbook. *You* haven't read it!" He grinned wickedly at Aleesa. She stuck her tongue out at him.

"Anyway," Kenneth went on. He lowered his voice. He didn't want anyone listening. They'd wonder how Kenneth had read about the present in a *textbook*.

"The chapter said a bunch of stuff. Some of the growers tried to make people think the union was Communist," he said. "Like Russia. You know." He leaned his head closer to Aleesa. "That scared people.

The growers said the workers were happy. They didn't want a union."

Aleesa snorted. "Right! The workers were treated great!" she said. Kenneth grinned at her.

"The growers said it was the Communists that started the strike. Not the workers," Kenneth whispered. "So everyone would be against the strike. And the boycott. But lots of priests and rabbis and ministers helped the union workers. They helped with the boycott and the strike. That changed people's minds."

"Well, I sure got treated like scum today," Aleesa snapped. "Communist or not." She frowned at Kenneth. "And when are we going to be able to get home, anyway?" she asked.

"Shhhh!" Kenneth said. Aleesa couldn't let anyone know they were from another time! What was wrong with her? "I don't know," he said in a whisper. "We will, somehow. We'll have to find that jug, I guess. But first we've got to help the union by stopping Luis. Don't you think?"

Kenneth looked around quickly. No one was listening. He turned back to Aleesa. "Luis might wreck the whole strike and boycott. The whole nonviolent movement. Who knows what might happen to the workers—and to *history* if we don't stop him?"

"*¡Bienvenidos!*" a voice said into a microphone. It was Chavez. Near him stood Dolores Huerta, another famous union leader.

Aleesa sat up straight. What was Chavez going to tell them? She glanced over her shoulder. Luis and his friends lounged against the wall at the back. Luis's face looked like he wanted to blow up every grower from here to Modesto. She shuddered.

"The boycott is working," Chavez was saying. "Other union workers are helping us. They are refusing to load grapes onto ships. People all over the U.S. aren't buying Schenley products. The strike is hurting the growers. Even though they bring in *braceros*. The strike is hurting them. We are having some success."

People began clapping. Chavez waited for the applause to die down. His face grew serious.

"But we are still threatened. The strike is costing the union thousands of dollars. We have to feed everyone. Luckily, people send money to feed us. We have to get up in the middle of the night to picket. And every day the growers harass us. They send the police to stop us. They follow us everywhere. They arrest us. We are pushed. We are shoved. Trucks try to run us down. They cover us with dirt. Many of us have black eyes, cut lips, and bandaged heads." Chavez gestured and walked up and down as he talked.

Aleesa watched the crowd. Their faces were intent on Chavez. People nodded in agreement. Everyone listened carefully. Chavez could really hold a crowd, she thought.

"They blast buckshot at our picket signs. They burn our signs. Today they tried to spray us with pesticide.

They claim it was an accident. Hah!" he exclaimed. He shook his head. "But still, the growers aren't giving up. Schenley still hasn't signed a contract with our union. So the union leaders have been talking." He looked over at Dolores Huerta. She smiled. "We have a new idea. One that will get everyone's attention. One that should force Schenley to sign."

Kenneth hunched forward in his seat. A hush fell over the crowd. What was Luis thinking now? he wondered. But he resisted the urge to look back at Luis.

"We will have a march," Chavez announced triumphantly. "A sacred pilgrimage. A *peregrinación*. We will march from here to Sacramento. We'll march 300 miles through the Central Valley. We'll march through all the small farming towns. Newspaper and TV reporters will be there too. We will arrive in Sacramento Easter Sunday. When we get there, we will have the attention of everyone in the country. We will meet with the Governor of California."

Kenneth sat up straighter. This really did sound like a good idea. And it was nonviolent too. Maybe this *would* change the growers' minds.

Chavez was still talking. "Everyone in the U.S. will know what a hard life we migrant workers have. They will force Schenley to sign for the union. *¡Nosotros venceremos!* We shall overcome, as my friend Martin Luther King Jr. says."

Everyone got up. They began to cheer loudly. Kenneth looked back at Luis. But he couldn't tell what Luis was thinking. Luis was talking to his friends. His fist waved in the air.

"Remember," Chavez said. "If we get full of anger, we can't think. If we can't think, we can't plan. If we can't plan, we can't win. *¡Viva La Causa! ¡Viva La Huelga!*" he exclaimed. Everyone cheered again. Feet stomped the ground. The building almost shook.

Kenneth raised his eyebrows at Aleesa. "What about Luis?" he asked in a whisper under the noise of the crowd. "Will he march?"

"I don't know," Aleesa said.

"But I want to march. Don't you?" Kenneth's words tumbled out. "Sure, Chavez said no kids could march. They'd be missing school. But we're already missing school—I guess. We'll just stay out of the way. No one will notice us. They'll be too busy. Just think! We could be part of history!" he said. His eyes glowed with excitement.

"I don't want to be part of history," Aleesa complained. "I want to go home." She sighed. "But, yeah, I'd like to go on the march too. If we have to be here. I really want the union workers—our friends—to win." She looked around her at the excited crowd.

Kenneth glanced back at Luis. "But Luis has to come too. We can't leave him in Delano," he said. "We don't know what he'll do."

"You're right," Aleesa said. They began to get up. Juan and Rosa got up too.

People crowded to the front of the hall. They were signing up for the march. Chavez was explaining things to people. Chavez knew what to do.

"So? What are we going to do?" Aleesa asked. She followed Kenneth through the crowd.

"We're going to convince Luis to come with us!" Kenneth said. His eyes crinkled up with a grin. He'd thought of it while Chavez was talking.

"What?" Aleesa almost shouted. "Luis wouldn't, would he?" She stared at Kenneth in disbelief.

"You watch," Kenneth said. "I've got an idea." Together they walked over to Luis.

"*¿Qué pasa?*" Luis asked. "What's up with you two? What do you think of Chavez's latest great idea that won't work?" He laughed and looked at his friends. His friends laughed too.

"We need to talk to you," Kenneth said. He glanced at Luis's friends. They didn't look too happy. Great. He took a deep breath. "Alone," he added.

Luis tossed his head "*¡Se vayan!*" he said to his friends. "*Hasta luego.*" They turned to leave. Then he looked at Kenneth and Aleesa. "This had better be good," he grumbled.

"Why don't you come on the march?" Kenneth asked. "You—"

"Hah!" Luis hooted. "On the march? You're crazy—
loco!" He threw his head back and laughed.

See? Aleesa wanted to say to Kenneth. But she bit her
tongue. Kenneth usually had a pretty good plan. Might as
well wait and find out.

Kenneth stayed calm. "No. Listen," he said. He bent
his head closer to Luis. "You really want to get back at
the growers. Right? The march is your answer. We'll be
marching through the whole Central Valley, right?"

"*Sí,*" Luis said grudgingly. He folded his arms across
his chest.

"Well, you heard Chavez. Reporters and TV cameras
will be there. Everyone in the U.S. will be watching."
Kenneth's voice got more excited. "You can get yourself
interviewed. Right on camera. You know how those TV
reporters are. They always want to talk to people who are
mad. And you're mad, aren't you?"

"That's right," Luis agreed. He unfolded his arms. He
hooked his thumbs through his belt loops. Aleesa could
tell he was thinking hard.

"Well, you can tell the TV audience what the growers
are really like!" Kenneth said. He looked at Luis's face. It
was like a mask. Was he making any sense?

Aleesa shot a glance at Kenneth. Was Kenneth crazy?
Wasn't this asking for trouble?

"Besides," Kenneth added. This was the hard part.
But he had to say it. "If you stay here and—ah—you do
something to get back at the growers—"

Luis's face grew dark. "I told you *silencio!*" he growled. He took a step toward Kenneth and Aleesa.

Now what was Kenneth doing? Aleesa wondered. He was going to get Luis mad again. This wasn't like him. Kenneth usually thought before he did something.

Kenneth cleared his throat nervously. "Ah—think about it. If you do something to the growers, they would try to stop the march. They'd want revenge for what *you* did here in Delano. Your parents will be marching. They might get hurt."

"Huh," Luis grunted. He looked down at the ground. "I hadn't thought of that," he said slowly. He looked up at the front of the hall. Kenneth and Aleesa followed his gaze. Dozens of workers were still signing up. Juan and Rosa were there too. They were smiling and gesturing excitedly.

"Not a bad idea," Luis added. "Maybe I'll go. Guess I'll sign us all up, right?" Luis said with a smile. "Maybe that's the best way. You two are okay after all."

Kenneth and Aleesa looked at each other. They grinned. "Yes!" they said at the same time. They watched Luis weave his way through the crowd.

They waited until Juan, Rosa, and Luis had finished signing. Then they walked out of the union hall into the street. It was already dark. The streetlights glowed in the fog. Mist swirled eerily. Workers got into their cars.

"*¡Hola!*" Luis said softly behind them. Kenneth and Aleesa turned. They ducked behind a car. They watched.

Luis motioned to his friends. His friends had been waiting outside for him.

"Uh, oh," Kenneth whispered. "Listen," he added. They strained their ears.

"—joke!" Luis was saying. "I'll go on the march, sure. But I'm not gonna talk to any *estupido* reporters. I'm going to—"

Just then, a car's engine started up. It sputtered, erasing Luis's last words to his friends.

"Great!" Kenneth said in a low voice to Aleesa. "What is Luis planning to do on the march?"

9

The Cops

"I can't believe it. It's almost time to march," Aleesa said to Kenneth. "This week has gone so fast! We start tomorrow!"

"Shhh!" Kenneth said. "I want to hear Senator Kennedy!" He leaned forward in his chair. "He came all this way. He wants to hear about migrant workers." He frowned at Aleesa.

Aleesa stuck her tongue out at him. "Fine," she said. "Who cares about a dumb old Senate hearing, anyway?" She slumped back down in her seat. She rested her chin in her hands.

Kenneth and Aleesa sat at the back of the crowded Delano High School Auditorium. Kenneth's heart beat faster. Senator Robert Kennedy was here in Delano. One of his heroes!

Some U.S. senators came to Delano. They came to the heart of farmworker country. They'd heard about farmworker problems. The NFWA strike got the senators' attention. Chavez also got their attention. The senators wanted to see for themselves. They wanted to hear people talk.

Kenneth had heard talk at the union all during the week. People had said the Senate might make some laws. The laws would help the workers have a union. This had been boring in his textbook. And Mrs. Carter made it even more boring. But being right here wasn't boring at all. Kenneth stared around him at the packed auditorium.

The auditorium was divided in half. On one side sat the growers and their friends. They had their arms crossed. They looked angry. On the other side sat farmworkers and union members. They wore *¡Huelga!* buttons and sombreros. They hunched forward on their seats. They were eager to hear everything. Kenneth could hear the soft sounds of someone turning the English into Spanish for a friend.

A grower was talking into a microphone. "The workers are happy! They don't want a union. We take care of them."

"Right!" Aleesa snorted next to him. She stared at Senator Kennedy. He was even better looking than on TV. And he really cared about people too. He was for civil rights. He was friends with Dr. Martin Luther King Jr. He fought for the blacks in the South. Maybe he would fight for migrant workers here too.

"He's cute," she whispered to Kenneth. "Maybe he'll—"

"Aleesa, pay attention," Kenneth broke in. He pointed to the front. Now the sheriff of Delano was speaking. Senator Kennedy was talking to him. "He's a big buddy of the growers," Kenneth said in a low voice.

"You mean, you arrested the picketers?" Senator Kennedy asked the sheriff. "Why?"

"Well, some of the vineyard workers were threatening the strikers. Said they'd cut out the hearts of the strikers," the sheriff said. "There was going to be a riot. So I had to arrest them."

Kenneth and Aleesa looked at each other. They'd heard Juan and Rosa talk about this. They still couldn't believe it.

"Wait," Senator Kennedy said. "These people were threatened with violence? But they were peacefully and lawfully exercising their rights?"

The sheriff was silent. The crowd sat still. Aleesa held her breath.

"Yet, you arrested the *victims* as the cause of trouble?" Kennedy leaned back in his chair. "I am stunned."

"They were ready to violate the law," the sheriff complained. He tugged his hat down lower on his forehead.

"I respectfully suggest that both the sheriff and the district attorney read the U.S. Constitution during the lunch break," Senator Kennedy snapped.

Cheering broke out. Kenneth and Aleesa clapped hard. They grinned at each other.

"With this *and* the march, we ought to win for sure!" Kenneth said.

"And the march begins tomorrow!" Aleesa exclaimed, her eyes bright.

The next morning Kenneth was up early. He looked at the newspaper headlines on the table in the union hall. All around him, people were talking excitedly. The big march to Sacramento was about to start.

Big banners flapped in the air. The flag of the NFWA stood tall. Large signs were everywhere. *¡Huelga!* and *¡Viva La Causa!* they read.

Cesar Chavez gave lists to people. Workers carried sacks of food. They packed sandwiches. They stuffed in extra socks. Newspaper and TV reporters hurried everywhere. Flashbulbs popped. Microphones crackled.

"Look, Aleesa," Kenneth said. He pointed to the headline. "Kennedy made the headlines. Now more people will know how wrong the growers are. The march has an even better chance of working. Schenley might sign a contract."

Aleesa read the words. Then she sighed. "I hope so. It's going to be a really long, long walk. Did you hear all the towns we're going into? Porterville, Fresno, Farmersville, Madera, Modesto, Stockton, and then Sacramento?" She slumped down on a chair. Was she really going to do this? "Why can't we march to Berkeley too? I want to go home," she said. She leaned over. She rubbed her feet. They already hurt. And she hadn't even started marching.

"We'll get there. I promise," Kenneth said. But how? he wondered silently. He could still see the blue jug of water with the letters BMS. Maybe it'd be back under the tree in Barker's vineyard. That's where they had to go again.

Or maybe they had to finish helping Cesar Chavez. Then maybe it'd magically appear. Would it? He gritted his teeth. Forget that for now, he told himself. They had something important to do right here.

"We have to help the union," Kenneth said. "We have to watch Luis." He narrowed his eyes. "We know he's got something planned. It could wreck everything. We're so close. And there are reporters everywhere watching. He can't ruin the march."

"Yeah," Aleesa said. "Knowing Luis, he might get crazy." She shook her head. Luis really did have a temper. Too bad. Usually he was a nice guy.

"*Vámonos,*" Chavez called out. Kenneth stood up. His pulse beat quickly. Here we go, he told himself.

Aleesa stood up too. Together, they followed the marchers out the door. They walked out into the sunshine.

At the head of the marchers, someone carried the U.S. flag. It fluttered in the wind. The NFWA black eagle floated proudly on its red flag too. Someone else carried the Mexican flag. Another, the Filipino flag. The Filipino workers had struck with their union. The banner of Our Lady of Guadalupe flapped in the breeze. Workers wore red hatbands with the black eagle on them. Everyone wore a red armband with a black eagle on it. Kenneth adjusted his proudly. So did Aleesa.

Everyone bowed heads. A priest prayed. Then everyone marched single file. They marched to the center of Delano. People lined the streets, cheering. Some tossed flowers at them. Others held signs saying *Viva La Causa!* A few swore at them. Growers' friends, Aleesa snorted to herself. Jerky labor contractors, probably.

"This is great!" Kenneth said. He grinned back at Aleesa. Chavez had told them to march single file. That was less threatening to people. Chavez and Dolores Huerta had planned out everything.

Chavez had people ready in each town on the route. They would feed the marchers. Some union people drove ahead in a car. They would drive to each town. They would find places to sleep. They'd look for places to have a rally. That way, more people would know about the march.

A volunteer nurse drove behind the marchers. She'd take care of anyone who was hurt. It was like fighting a war, Kenneth told himself. But it was a peaceful war. Other union people were going to stay behind in Delano. They'd keep picketing. Dolores Huerta would stay behind.

A voice shouted through a bullhorn. "Where do you think you're going?"

Kenneth blinked. He looked ahead. When he saw, he almost froze. Then he looked back wildly for Aleesa. Whew. She was still behind him. She stood stock still. Her eyes widened.

"Oh, no!" she moaned softly. She stared ahead of the line. Her veins turned to ice. This was horrible.

The Delano police force stood in the sun. Their arms were linked solidly. They blocked Garces, the main street. The guns in their holsters gleamed.

Aleesa swallowed hard. Police cars, their lights flashing, blocked the street behind them. Snarling police dogs on leashes barked.

"You must disband. You cannot march," the police chief shouted through his bullhorn. "You have no permit. This is illegal!"

Kenneth stared. The police looked big. And they looked angry. Angry! Uh, oh. Where was Luis? Kenneth looked ahead of him. There was Luis looking furious. Great. What would he do now? He could ruin everything.

The marchers bunched together. They all stopped talking. Some marchers dropped to their knees. They began praying. But Cesar Chavez looked calm. Aleesa crowded next to Kenneth.

She could see news reporters talking into their tape recorders. The red lights on the TV cameras were on. Cameras clicked again and again.

"I don't like this," she whispered. Her heart beat under her shirt. Would Chavez finally get angry?

Kenneth swallowed hard. "Me either," he whispered back.

"Kenneth, how about Luis?" she asked worriedly.

They watched Luis carefully. Now he crouched on the curb next to some of his friends. He scowled.

"I don't know," Kenneth said. He tensed. "We'll just have to watch him. If he starts to get up, we'll have to grab him, quick," he said.

"Oh, sure," Aleesa moaned. She rubbed her forehead.

They waited in the sun. The marchers talked quietly.

The Cops

Chavez was talking to the police chief. Then another man in a suit got out of a car. He joined the two men. They all talked. The reporters crowded in closer. And everyone waited.

Flags hung still in the air. Police radios blared. The police still stood blocking the street.

Chavez came back to the marchers. He spoke softly. Kenneth and Aleesa listened. Everyone was silent.

"They are deciding," Chavez said. "Remember, hatred saps strength and energy. We need our strength. We need our energy."

Kenneth took a quick look at Luis. He looked as if he was listening hard.

"We need our strength and energy to win. Hatred will cause our defeat. We need discipline and strength. Remember!" Chavez looked at the face of each marcher. "We can turn the world around if we do it nonviolently."

Kenneth saw Luis rest his chin on his fist. Luis tightened his mouth. What was he thinking?

Finally, "You're free to go," the police chief growled. The marchers and the gathered crowd cheered.

"Yes!" Aleesa crowed. She grinned at Kenneth. "Chavez did it, somehow!"

The marchers got back into their single-file line. Cheering, they began the march again. Ahead, Kenneth could see Luis marching. His shoulders looked set. Was Luis still planning to do something?

The police had tried to stop them in their own town. What other dangers lay ahead of them on the march? He'd heard terrible stories of what might happen. What growers were planning.

And what would Luis do then? Would that be the end of the peaceful march? And what about everything Chavez had worked so hard for?

10

The Way to Win

"We're almost to Stockton," Kenneth called back to Aleesa. "That's almost to Sacramento!"

Aleesa wiped her forehead. She raised a hand. Almost, she thought. Almost. That wasn't good enough.

Kenneth looked down at his shoes. His feet were tired. He had blisters. His back ached. Even football practice didn't seem as hard as this. But then, this was the nineteenth day of the march. He couldn't believe he was still doing this.

They'd marched about 15 miles a day. The farm country was flat. Dusty roads, hot sun, even in March and April. They'd camped by campfires at night. Priests said mass every morning. Rabbis and ministers marched with them too.

Reporters came. Everyone in the U.S. knew about the march, it seemed. Lots of people wanted the migrant workers to win. People brought them food, flowers, and clean socks. Many people had helped.

Kenneth shoved his hands into his pockets. There had been no bad trouble—yet. Everyone had listened to Chavez.

Kenneth frowned. Even Luis—so far. But Schenley still hadn't signed a union contract either. The union still hadn't won. When would Luis do something about it? He felt his muscles tighten. He had a bad feeling.

He looked ahead. The flags still flew. The first marchers still held them. Cesar Chavez limped along. Chavez's ankle had swollen. Kenneth had seen it. Chavez's back was in pain. But Chavez kept going. He was a strong man, Kenneth thought.

Just behind Kenneth, Aleesa sighed. She watched her feet trudge on the dirt shoulder of the highway. They'd marched over 200 miles. She shook her head. She couldn't believe it. She couldn't believe she was doing this.

Would they ever be able to get home? Would she be a migrant worker forever? No way, she thought, frowning. That just couldn't be.

Kenneth dropped back. He grinned at Aleesa.

"What do you think will happen when we get to Stockton?" he asked. "That's a pretty big city." He slowed his pace to match hers.

"I just want to lie down. I just want to sleep," Aleesa said. She brushed her hair from her eyes. "I just want to go home," she added.

"Do you think there'll be mariachi bands and all that stuff? Like in Fresno?" Kenneth asked. "The people there were nice," he added. "Remember how they marched along with us through the city? The mayor even welcomed us. He had cops help us out."

"Yeah," Aleesa said. She looked across the highway at a ranch house. It was set back from the road. A sign sat on a card table in front of the house. *We buy Schenley products!* it said. Bottles and cans stood next to it. Across one window hung a sign. *Commie union strikers go home!* Aleesa pointed across the road.

"Look at that," she said. "Another friend of a grower." She frowned. "Some people just don't care about the farmworkers. We've seen too many of those signs on this march. And people yelling stuff at us. And throwing things too. Dogs tried to attack us even. Remember?"

Kenneth looked back in the line. Luis still marched, along with two of his friends. The others had gone back to Delano in a car. Rosa and Juan marched near the end of the line.

"Uh huh. We're lucky that Luis hasn't done anything yet," he said in a low voice. "Lucky that Chavez or someone else has always been around. They've handled problems okay. Luis hasn't had a chance to make trouble."

Kenneth shaded his eyes with his hand. He stared back again. He still had that feeling nagging him. Luis would lose control somehow. And then what would happen to their cause?

There were so many reporters around. Every day. The trouble Luis made would be in all the papers. Everyone would get mad. The union would lose. And the growers would win.

"Yet. No problems *yet*," Aleesa reminded him.

Ranch houses became closer together. More cars roared by. *Stockton–1 mile* read a green sign by the side of the road.

"What's that?" Kenneth asked. He pointed ahead. "Look!"

At the front of the line, dozens of cars had stopped by the side of the road. People were piling out of the cars. They were smiling and cheering.

"*¡Bienvenidos!*" Chavez was saying. He turned to the line of marchers. "These *amigos* are going to march with us!"

Shouts and cheers rang out. Within half an hour, hundreds of people had joined them. Hundreds more waited, cheering, in the city.

Crowds lined the main streets. Kenneth's jaw dropped. Mariachi bands played. People stood, holding signs. *Good luck, NFWA!* and *¡Viva La Huelga!* and *¡Viva La Causa!* the signs read.

"Look, Aleesa," Kenneth said. He pointed to people standing on the curb. Workers from other unions lined the curbs. They held signs too. "Glaziers and asbestos workers," he read. "Everyone is with us!" he exclaimed.

"Oh, yeah?" a voice said behind them. "So then, why aren't we winning?" Kenneth and Aleesa turned around. It was Luis. He marched along, his hands shoved angrily into his pockets.

"We're almost to Sacramento," Luis said. "The march is all over the papers. TV stations too. People are telling Schenley to sign a union contract. And Schenley isn't signing. The growers aren't backing down. The march is worthless. The strike is worthless."

Luis spit on the ground. Aleesa jumped. Kenneth tossed her a look. Aleesa had to calm down, he thought.

"I listened to Chavez. I believed him," Luis went on. He took his hands out of his pockets. Then he slammed a fist into an open hand. "But now I'm not so sure," he finished. He looked at Kenneth and Aleesa. His eyebrows knit into an angry frown.

"We can't know yet," Kenneth said. "Chavez said to be patient," he added. Luis sure looked angry. Change the subject, Kenneth told himself.

"Look, we're almost to the park for our rally," Kenneth said. He pointed to the sign that read *St. Mary's Park*. Balloons flew in the air. People cheered. Signs bobbed up and down. The trumpets from a mariachi band played a brisk tune.

"This is the best one—" Kenneth began. Then he stopped. His heart thudded.

Oh, no! Aleesa said to herself. She stared.

A big man wearing a tan shirt stood in their way. His eyes glinted evilly at the three of them.

"Communists! Lazy Chicanos!" he shouted. He folded his beefy arms. "If you want to get to your rally, you'd better hurry," he taunted. He planted his boots firmly. He stood across the sidewalk.

Fear raced through Kenneth. His mind was spinning. What could they do? He felt Aleesa's gaze on him.

Aleesa felt her stomach flip. What was this guy going to do? This was just like in those awful movies they had to watch in social studies. She heard the click of a camera. She turned her head.

Oh great, she moaned to herself. A reporter stood watching, a few feet away. Two more reporters walked up quickly. One had a TV camera. If there was going to be a fight, they would probably plaster it all over the news. No more peaceful march. No more union—they'd lose.

She elbowed Kenneth. He whipped his head around. His eyes widened when he saw the reporters.

"Hey you—" Luis began angrily. He took a step forward.

This was the worst, Kenneth thought. This was going to wreck the whole march. He reached out a hand to grab Luis.

Just then, the big man spit. The spittle lay on the cement, right in front of Luis's work boots.

Kenneth and Aleesa gasped together. Then Kenneth grabbed Luis's shoulder. Maybe he could steady him, he hoped.

"We hate all you Chicanos," the man shouted. He wiped his mouth with his hand.

Think! Kenneth told himself. Just like on the football field. How are you going to save the game? What could he do? "Hate, hate, hate!" the man's words echoed in his brain.

That was it. His answer. Chavez's words.

"Hate?" Kenneth asked quickly. "Hatred is bad for you," he said. His pulse pounded in his forehead. His fingers dug into Luis's shoulder. Aleesa stiffened next to him.

Suddenly, Luis straightened up. He glared at the man.

"Yeah," Luis said tightly. "Hatred will make you lose. That's why *we* will win." He tossed his hair out of his eyes. "You growers—you don't treat us with dignity. But we will win our rights. We won't fight you. We'll save our strength. We are stronger. We will win."

The reporters wrote quickly. The TV camera blinked its red light. Kenneth let his breath out. Aleesa grabbed his arm. The big man looked confused.

"Now, we're going to join our *hermanos!*" Luis said. "*¡Viva La Causa!*" he said.

He linked arms with Kenneth and Aleesa. Together, the three of them walked around the big man. He stood puzzled, looking after them. The reporters walked away.

"All right, Luis!" Kenneth shouted when they'd left the man behind. They threaded their way through the crowd.

"Way to go, Luis!" Aleesa echoed. She grinned at Kenneth. All around them, crowds pushed, trying to find a place to sit.

"I thought you were going to start a fight," Kenneth said. His mouth was still dry. "Why didn't you?" he asked Luis.

Kenneth led Luis and Aleesa around a group of reporters. The three dropped down on the grass in front of a bandstand. Flags stood on the stage. A band played loudly.

Luis looked a little sheepish. He stared down at the grass. "Well," he said. "I heard you say that hatred was bad." He stopped. He looked at both Kenneth and Aleesa. "That made me remember what Chavez said. About hatred taking away our strength. And that's what the growers want. They want us to hate. They want us weak." Luis began to smile. "So I decided to stay strong."

Kenneth and Aleesa smiled at each other. "Good work, Kenneth," Aleesa said.

"Yeah, thanks," Kenneth said. "But Luis did the right thing," he added.

"*¡Sí!*" Luis said. "For once," he finished with a grin.

People had been making announcements on the bandstand. Suddenly a cheer rose up from the crowds in the park. Now Chavez stood up. He was smiling broadly. He was holding a piece of paper.

"*¡Hermanos!* Brothers and sisters! I have a wonderful announcement to make." He held the paper up.

Kenneth and Aleesa looked at each other. Was this it? Had it finally happened? Kenneth wondered.

"Tomorrow we make our final steps on the march to Sacramento. But I will not be with you."

The crowd murmured. People called out.

"*¿Porqué?*"

"*¿Porqué no, Cesar?*"

"I've just had an important phone call," Chavez said into the mike. "The lawyer for Schenley says they want to sign! A union contract! The NFWA has won!"

"Yes!" Kenneth and Aleesa yelled together. Luis grinned.

The crowd roared. They were on their feet. Yelling and shouting filled the air.

"*¡Viva! ¡Viva! ¡Viva La Causa!*"

"We won! We won!"

"*¡Viva La Huelga!*"

"We helped too," Kenneth said to Aleesa. He couldn't stop grinning.

Her eyes shone. "We did. We really did!"

Kenneth saw something on the grass from the corner of his eye. Something blue.

"Aleesa!" he yelled in her ear. He reached down. The jug—the blue jug! He turned it around quickly. On the side it read *BMS*.

"Yes!" she screeched. "That's it! That's gotta be it!"

Kenneth hurriedly twisted off the cap. He let the water run down his throat. Then he handed it to Aleesa. She shut her eyes. The cool water felt good.

She opened her eyes. She blinked. Kenneth felt a shiver. He looked around him.

The cheering crowd, Luis, the banners, the band, Cesar Chavez—all had vanished! He and Aleesa knelt in a flower bed under an oak tree. The buildings of Berkeley Middle School surrounded them.

"What have you two slackers been doing?" a voice barked behind them. Mr. Moody.

"Oh, hi, Mr. Moody!" Kenneth said. He grinned. He thought he'd never been so happy to see that jerk.

"Yeah, hi, Mr. M.," Aleesa chimed in. Mr. Moody! She almost wanted to hug him.

"Why be so cheerful? Better get to work," Mr. Moody snapped. "Mrs. Carter won't be happy if you don't finish." He stalked off.

"We're back! We're home!" Aleesa whispered excitedly.

"Finally," Kenneth said. He watched Mr. Moody's back disappear into the building.

"Did it really happen?" Aleesa asked. She crinkled her forehead. "Mr. Moody didn't seem to think we'd been anywhere. Was it a dream?" she asked slowly. "It couldn't have been, could it? Do you know what I'm talking about?"

Kenneth paused for a moment. Then he reached his arm out. He grabbed Aleesa's arm. "Look," he said, pointing with his other hand.

Aleesa stared. On their arms, they still wore the red armbands. The black eagle spread its wings proudly on the red cloth.

"¡*Viva La Causa!*" Kenneth whispered, smiling.

"¡*Viva La Causa!*" Aleesa echoed.

They grinned at each other and picked up their weed diggers.

"Now I can't wait for the social studies test," Aleesa said. "I'm gonna get an A—and Grandma will pass out!"

"No kidding," Kenneth said. "So will Mrs. Carter. We'll both get A's. And we'll never forget this."

"Never," said Aleesa.

"Get moving," Mr. Moody's voice shouted at them from his office window. "Lucky you don't work in the vineyards. You two jokers don't even know what real hard work is!"

"Hah!" Aleesa and Kenneth said together.

And they broke out laughing.

Cesar Chavez

For Cesar Chavez, a farm was always home. He was born on March 31, 1927, on his parents' small farm in Arizona. They were poor but proud. They owned their own land. They grew corn, vegetables, and alfalfa. Cesar and his family were happy to work for themselves. They were glad they owed money to no one. They had enough food.

But then the Depression came. Everyone had big money troubles. In the cities, people lost jobs. Thousands of farmers lost their farms. The Chavez family began to owe people money. When Cesar was about ten, the sheriff came to their small farm. "You must leave," he said. "Leave or else go to jail. You owe too many taxes. You can't stay here anymore."

Cesar and his brothers and sisters were worried and confused. His parents packed the family car. They had to leave a lot behind. While they drove away, Cesar watched a bulldozer crawl over their land. It knocked down the fences they used to swing on. He couldn't believe it.

Now the Chavez family had nothing. Like many other families, they drove west. They hoped to find work in California. If they could find a farm, they could work for the farmer. The Chavez family drove wherever there was a crop they could pick. They picked grapes, vegetables, cotton, and carrots all over California.

FIGHT IN THE FIELDS: CESAR CHAVEZ

It was hard work. They picked from sunup to sundown. Many times, they wouldn't get paid. They would get cheated out of their money. The Chavez family had to live in run-down shacks like all the other migrant workers. They often could not go to school and had to pick instead. Cesar changed schools more than 30 times. The Chavez family struggled all the time.

Cesar realized that something had to change. He knew what it was like to have been free and to have dignity. But a migrant worker had no freedom or dignity. The labor contractor and the grower had all the power. Many times, they paid the workers as little as they could get away with. Often, they made the workers live in filthy shacks. Workers even had to pay for a drink of water while they worked. Many other people treated Mexican Americans badly only because of their race. The Mexican American migrant workers had a hard, hard life. Cesar promised himself he would change that.

At 17, Cesar joined the U.S. Navy. There he found other people hurt too. He realized people are all basically the same inside.

After the Navy, Cesar went back to picking because he had only an eighth grade education. But he was proud of being one of the best pickers. He married his wife, Helen, in 1948. In the next years, they had five children.

In the 1950s, Cesar went to work for the CSO. The Community Services Organization was a group formed to help Mexican Americans. The CSO helped them register to vote. They drove people to the hospital. They got roads paved. They tried to stop police from bothering the Mexican Americans.

Life was getting worse for migrant farmworkers. The *bracero* program, which brought in workers from Mexico, was keeping wages down. The *braceros* would work for very little money. So the growers and labor contractors hired only people who would work cheaply. No one could get work that paid. Finally, Cesar decided to form a union for farmworkers.

From the first strike against the grape growers in 1965 to the strike against the lettuce growers to his death in 1993, Cesar Chavez worked for the migrant workers. He made little money. He took no time for himself. He lived in a small house. But his family was proud of him. They helped him with the union movement. Thousands looked up to him for his ways.

Because of Cesar Chavez, the union won a minimum wage for workers. Now growers had to pay a minimum. They couldn't cheat the farmworkers. Work conditions were safer too. Migrant workers found new dignity because of Cesar Chavez.

Cesar Chavez never fought back against anyone who hurt him. He thought fighting with fists was weak. He believed with Dr. Martin Luther King Jr. that nonviolence was the key to winning. He was right.

FIGHT IN THE FIELDS: CESAR CHAVEZ

The farmworkers' union, the UFW, helps farmworkers live decent lives. Without Cesar Chavez, they would be struggling still.